Pa

Memories

Written and Illustrated
By Risa Tham

ISBN: 9798700427296

Printed by Amazon Direct Publishing.

I would like to thank the Lord for being with me and my family who had supported and guided me in my journey of writing this book.

I would also like to thank Young Author Academy for giving me the opportunity of publishing this book.

This book is dedicated to all those who I share cherished memories with, and to all those who help me make wonderful memories every day.

Contents

Chapter One

Summer Vacation Begins

"1...2...3...go!"

Paper airplanes flew across the sky, as five kids watched them with glee, happy to see that their 'hard work' in making them had paid off.

Irene, one of the kids with short hair and chestnut brown eyes, looked at the gliding paper planes and thought she was at her happiest.

Then the boy with black hair and deep black eyes, who sat next to her, said softly, "Today's the last day we all get to hang out like this together. And to come to think of it, these paper planes look like they carry off all those memories we made, but they don't return to us, do they?

These good old times will soon be gone, just like they do, and who knows, will the memories fade away too?" He looked at Irene, but she couldn't answer him.

Deep in thought, Irene turned to look at all of her other friends, and, one by one, they disappeared. "No...Wait!" She tried calling out to them but she couldn't hear herself speak.

As she was about to make sense of what was happening, a voice called out to her, "Irene...wake up...WAKE UP!"

Irene opened her eyes slowly, rubbing them before she looked around at her surroundings. "Where am I..." she groaned.

"Come on Irene. We're still in class, but thankfully the last period is finally over. We're all tired because this semester was really stressful, but today's the last day before summer vacation starts, and you know what that means right?" Irene glanced at the person talking to her.

"Oh it's you, Yukine... Summer vacation?" She slowly sat back up. Then it hit her. "SUMMER VACATION! I'M GOING HOME!"

She stood up in a hurry and packed her things. Yukine giggled as she watched her. "That took you a while... must have had a nice dream. You had such a happy grin on your face while you napped that even I was of two minds whether to wake you up or not."

Upon hearing this, Irene paused her packing for a while, then smiled softly as she went back to work. "A dream huh?...well I guess so..."

The very next day, Irene was at the airport waving goodbye to her best friend Yukine, before rushing into the busy crowd waiting in line to board their airplanes.

Irene was an international undergraduate student in Japan, and was therefore going back to her homeland situated in the lush green hills of the eastern Himalayas in India. The place she calls home is in the province of Meghalaya.

Yukine though, being Japanese, had only come to see her off. "I'll miss you! Take care and bring me some souvenirs from your hometown!"

"I sure will! Take care of yourself as well! See you next semester!" Irene replied.

It was a long flight back home, and a three hour car journey from the nearest international airport where the plane landed. Throughout the journey, Irene was pretty much quiet, still thinking about her dream that she had a few days prior and her childhood friends whom she was about to see. She had not seen them since she left for Japan which was after middle school for her higher studies, and was only in contact with her best friend, Camie and her brother, Daniel.

The rain poured and a nostalgic feeling was in the air as she approached her hometown, Shillong. "Kenma, Camie, Daniel, and Hame...I wonder what you all are up to right now?" The rain stopped just in time for her to get out near Golf Links, a golf course, a popular hangout and picnic spot in her hometown, and just close enough to her house.

She got out of the taxi and just stood there, looking around the golf courses, with baggage and all. She checked her messages and calls, mumbling, "Where are they?"

Then she decided to walk across the golf course to take a short cut back home.

'Thank goodness there are only a few people here at this time of day,' She thought as she dragged her suitcases behind her. Just halfway across the golf course, she saw someone who seemed to be running towards her. She first walked on, but then stopped as the figure appeared closer to her, one that seemed familiar to her. "Wait, that couldn't be her, could it?" But it was all too familiar. Light brown hair with golden highlights, tied in low pony tails, light brown eyes and that high pitched voice which called out her name. "I can't be mistaken...it's really you... Camie!"

Chapter Two
Incomplete Reunion

"I thought you had forgotten that we had planned to meet up!" Irene said as she hugged her childhood best friend with happy tears in her eyes.

"Of course I wouldn't girl, what do you take me for?" Camie replied as she returned her hug, laughing.

"Irene!" Someone called in the distance. Irene looked ahead and saw two other people waving their hands as they walked to them. Recognising them immediately, Irene called out, "Daniel! Hame! You guys came too!"

"Of course we did! It's been too long since we all met up right? Hmm...Since Middle School, if I'm not mistaken," Hame replied.

"And I can't say no to Camie when she insists upon certain things or else there would be no peace in the house for days," Daniel said, while dodging his sister's punch.

Laughter filled the air as they helped Irene with her bags and suitcases and walked her home. Once home, Irene greeted her family, who were eagerly waiting for her arrival.

After hugs, kisses and stories were exchanged, Irene and her friends enjoyed some tea and then headed off to her room. It was a nostalgic feeling for her to be back home in her own room. They kept all her bags and baggage in the corner and sat down to catch up with each other.

Camie and her brother Daniel, were currently studying in Chennai, a city of Southern India, while Hame was doing his undergraduate studies from Shillong itself.

It was fun hearing stories and experiences from each other while chewing on snacks and drinking carbonated juice. However, the laughter soon died down, and everyone could feel that it was time to bring up the topic that was pushed to the side. It wasn't avoidable, but painful to talk about. Seeing the silence that had prevailed for quite some time, Irene took a deep breath and let out a sigh, before she began to speak.

"Kenma... has any of you heard from him?"

Flashback, 10 years prior....

"Pass me the ball, Irene!"

"Here, try to score this time Daniel!"

"Hah! You guys won't be able to get through me as long as I'm the goal keeper!"

"We'll see about that...pass me the ball Daniel."

The ball rolled from one corner to the other of the soccer field. Hame rushed to the front of the goal and tried to score, but Camie managed to block that as well, and the ball went rolling to the other corner of the field.

That's when someone came running in, dribbled the ball right to the goal and gave it one big kick to score. It flew into the air, went past Camie's almost unbreakable defence and right into the net.

Surprised, everyone turned to look at who it was. The boy with black hair and deep and mysterious eyes then turned to them with a smile and gave a little bow.

"Sorry for interrupting the match just now. I'm Kenma... I've just shifted here with my parents from Japan recently, and I was really hoping to find some friends here."

Silence followed, but soon the sound of clapping filled the air.

"Wow Kenma, that was one good shot right there! Nice to meet you! I'm Daniel."

"Impressive! You were the only one who was able to get past me today...I'm Camie!"

"Sorry, you had to see me failing to score for the 15th time today...I'm Hame." Irene gave a big smile and held out her hand.

"You were so cool! I'm Irene, and looks like you've just made a bunch of friends Kenma!"

PRESENT:

More silence followed, before Hame spoke up. "Well, as you all may know, Kenma left for Japan to visit his grandparents around six months after you did. His parents left for Japan a few months later to check up on the situation there. However, since then, no one has come back."

Camie then followed up, saying, "Kenma went offline from his social media due to some exam he was taking, but never went online again. We all have tried to contact him, but he has not responded to our messages or mails."

More silence followed.

"I just heard recently that there had been an incident that took place in his family, but I have no clue about it," Irene said.

Camie then clenched her fists and said, "He came into our lives as a surprise that day, and became one of us so quickly. There is no way he was ever given permission to just walk out in surprise though!"

Daniel kept his hand on his sister's shoulder and shook his head, trying to calm her down.

"You don't think-" Irene didn't want to complete the sentence. She didn't have to.

All of them had thought of it, but no one wanted to say it out loud. All they could do was hope and pray that nothing dreadful had happened to Kenma or his family.

Chapter Three

Summer Surprises at a Book Stall

After the silence that prevailed as they thought about what could have happened to Kenma, Irene started a conversation to remember and relive the times they all had fun together in the past.

There was a hint of sadness and worry amongst everyone whenever Kenma was brought up, but it was mostly covered up with soft smiles of gratitude and reminiscence as they remembered their adventures and the enjoyable moments that they had had. After a few more stories and plans for the rest of the vacation, they decided to leave.

Irene saw her friends out, freshened up, and then spent the rest of the evening with her family, telling them about her experiences in college, her friends, her difficulties and challenges, and her successes.

After dinner, Irene and her younger sister, Caitlyn, spent time catching up with each other, sharing secrets, and playing games until Caitlyn felt somnolent. Irene then tucked her sister in bed, said goodnight to her parents, and headed off to her room, tired after the day's travel.

As she lay in bed, she turned to her side table where she had kept pictures of her loved ones. Her eyes rested on the picture of herself, Camie, Daniel, Hame, and Kenma. "Kenma... our friendship circle will not be complete without you...where are you?" She said to herself in a quiet and soft voice filled with sadness, concern, and worry. Slowly, she drifted off to sleep.

"These paper planes look like they carry all those memories we made, but they don't return to us, do they? These good old times will soon be gone, just like they do, and who knows, will the memories fade away too?"

"Huh...what do you mean Kenma?"

"Oh it's nothing..." The small smile at the end, both mysterious and full of understanding that Irene and the others weren't able to catch.

"Kenma, what did you mean... I wonder..."

Then suddenly Kenma appeared with the others, waving goodbye at the airport. From the aeroplane's window, she could see her friends, but Kenma suddenly turned around, grabbed onto a huge paper plane, and flew far into the horizon, his figure getting smaller and smaller.

With both hands on the window, she watched helplessly as he disappeared from her sight. She took a deep breath, ready to call out to him. "Kenma!"

Irene looked around. She wasn't on an aeroplane; she was in her room, sitting straight up on her bed. "It was just a dream..." She said with a sigh of relief.

But she wasn't able to make sense of it, because she had happened to gaze right upon the clock's face.

"IT'S 9 AM!" The sudden realization of how late she had gotten up made her quickly launch out of her bed, change into some home clothes and head off to the bathroom to freshen up. Everyone else in her family had woken up hours ago, so she quickly ran downstairs to have her breakfast, wishing her family good morning along the way.

After breakfast, it was time for her chores. She would usually dislike doing them, but being away from home for so long made her quite happy to do them. Then they were followed by her workout, a bath, and then lunch.

At the lunch table, she asked her mom, "Mom, can I visit grandfather in his bookstall and maybe help around there?"

"Of course dear, but are you sure it isn't also because you want to browse for books there? You always did that when you were young, with your friends and all. And I remember you and one of your other friends would always beg your grandfather for some books to carry back home," Irene's mom said with a laugh.

"Oh you mean me and...Kenma..." Irene then looked down at her plate.

"Oh yes, he's the one. Your Japanese friend right? I heard that he went back to Japan a few years back... did you meet him there?" Irene started fidgeting with some of the peas on her plate when she heard her mom's question. Thankfully, she was saved by the doorbell.

"It must be your dad...well I'm going to go with your sister and your dad today to attend some meeting at her school. You can take a cab and visit your grandfather after we leave."

"Okay Mom, thanks!" Irene said with relief, grateful that she had avoided talking about Kenma.

A few hours later, a taxi dropped Irene off at her grandfather's shop. She went in and walked around the shop, only to see her cousin, brother and one of her grandfather's old employees.

"Hey there cousin Irene! Good to see you back!"

"Hey Nathaniel! I've missed you! And my, you've grown!"

They exchanged their special handshake routine as they both laughed.

"Have you heard? I'm headed off for college next year...Right now though, I just help grandpa whenever I can these days because I'm having my summer vacation, and because his other employee went back to his village to attend to some family business."

"That's amazing news, Nathaniel! Congratulations on getting into college!" Irene said happily.

Nathaniel grinned. "Thanks a lot Irene. Anyways, if you're searching for grandpa, he left for home to get grandma some medicines for her sore throat, but he'll be back soon."

"Oh I see... well I suggest you let me take over things here as I wait for grandpa, while you can have a break in the meantime."

Irene then proceeded to put her things away and stood at the counter. Nathaniel handed her some keys to locked bookcases and gave a quick recap on what she had to do.

"Thanks Irene! I'll be going then."

Nathaniel waved to her as he left the shop. It had been a few minutes, and there weren't many potential customers to be seen. So, Irene decided to browse through some books. "I knew grandpa had it... the fifth volume to the Manga that I'm reading!" She happily took the manga out and stood back at the counter, reading the Manga and looking up every now and then to see if any customers came in.

While she was reading, the shop's doors opened. "Welcome to David's Bookstore!" Irene greeted the customer with her usual cherry smile.

"Glad to be here," the customer responded.

"That voice! Where have I heard it?" She blinked her eyes a few times as she looked at who her customer was. Her eyes widened in surprise and disbelief as she stared at the figure in front of her. Standing in front of her was the very person she least expected to see, but longed the most to see again. Dark black hair, and deep and mysterious black eyes. It had been a few years, but she would always be able to recognize that small smile and gentle voice anywhere. With tears welling up in her eyes, Irene said with a quivering voice, "It's y-you...it's you, isn't it...Kenma...I-I can't believe it...You're finally here."

Chapter Four
The Mystery Unfolds

"Kenma..." The very name Irene thought that she wasn't going to call out anytime soon was falling right of her mouth as she stared with a mixture of disbelief and joy at the person in front of her.

He looked at her, surprised as well, and then said to her, "You know my name... Have we met miss?"

"Is this a trick question? He can't be serious..." Irene thought confused as she cleared her throat. "Come on Kenma... I know it's been a few years, but I really haven't changed that much, certainly not enough for you to forget me right?" She said with worry creeping in as she saw the blank expression on his face.

"Irene..." he repeated, with an expression of deep thought, as if he was trying to remember something.

"Oh Irene!" He suddenly exclaimed.

Irene, who was waiting for his reply anxiously, breathed out a sigh of relief. A little too soon, however, Kenma smiled at her, and said, "You're the one from the picture back home... one of my childhood friends right?"

Irene was about to nod and say yes when she realized something, "What do you mean a picture...and of course I'm one of your childhood friends...Kenma...what is happening?"

Irene was too shocked and confused to say anything more. Kenma looked at her, and then realized something as well. He looked away with a sad expression on his face. "What should I do?...Should I approach him?...Is this even him?...the Kenma we knew back then..."

Questions piled up in Irene's mind, that she just stood there, frozen still with confusion and shock.

Then suddenly, the doors opened once more, and in came a tall and gorgeous looking woman, having similar features to Kenma, and who looked very familiar to Irene. Waking in with an air of confidence, she turned to Kenma and said, "So, have you found the manga you wanted to buy?

..Or are you lost in looking at other books as always?"

"Huh? Oh no Chisaki-san...um...I just happened to meet one of my friends from here...she's the one looking after the shop" Kenma replied nervously.

"Childhood friend?" Chisaki looked over at Irene, who still wore the expression of confusion and disbelief. Then she came to realize the situation they were in.

She gave a little sigh, and then beckoned Kenma to follow her to the counter where Irene was standing. As they approached her, Irene woke up from her swirling thoughts and greeted them with a forced smile.

Before she could say anything, Chisaki held her hand up to stop her and said, "I apologize for Kenma's strange behavior...I'm Chisaki, his older cousin sister. I know that not many people knew about what happened to him, and you must be one of them....I don't know if you remember this, but when you guys were kids, I had stayed over to watch over Kenma while his parents were on a business trip."

Finally, Irene could remember why she seemed so familiar to her. Vague flashbacks of Chisaki dropping Kenma off to play with them and sometimes she would stay and play with them as well flashed before her eyes. Irene nodded slowly.

Chisaki grinned. "Alright, now that that is out of the way, would you like for me to tell you about the incident?"

Irene slowly nodded her head again as she looked over at Kenma who was looking at the ground and fidgeting his fingers nervously.

To make him more comfortable, Irene said, "Whatever may have happened, and whatever reason there was to why we never knew what had happened to him, I'm just glad...glad to see him a-again." Irene's last few words quivered as tears welled up her eyes.

Kenma looked at her, surprised, and then smiled reassuringly. Chisaki smiled as well, and then began to tell her about what had happened. "You must have known that Kenma left here a few years back to visit his grandparents. During that time, he was also preparing himself for a high-school entrance exam to one of Okinawa's high-schools, as he and his parents had agreed to continue his further studies nearer to his grandparents place, owing to grandfather's health condition that time. Of course, he would have never left without a goodbye, and he was planning to return to Shillong and say his farewell to his close ones back here." Chisaki's face then darkened. "However, on the very day he got his results, in which he had done pretty well, he excitedly ran back to inform his family about them.

While he crossed the road, he didn't see a car driving beyond the speed limit heading towards him. That's when the accident happened. We're just so thankful that it wasn't very serious and that the driver didn't just leave him there. He and a group of people were fast enough to call for an ambulance, and he reached the hospital in time. However, he did suffer from some sprains, a few broken bones, and an amnesia attack, which he hasn't fully recovered from."

Irene listened to all of this, horrified, but at the same time relieved that Kenma was able to recover from most of the injuries.

Then it struck her. "The amnesia attack... is this why he couldn't remember me earlier?" She asked.

Chisaki nodded her head. "Sadly, he hasn't fully recovered from his amnesia yet, especially when it comes to his memories here. That is why we couldn't contact anyone back here. His parents left in a hurry just as they heard the news, and after he recovered from physical injuries, he wasn't able to recall passwords to his accounts, and his phone was beyond repair after the accident."

Irene took a deep breath to try to process what she had heard. That's when Kenma spoke up.

"This bookstore... I'm getting a sense of deja vu... did I come here often?"

Irene eyes lit up as she heard this. "Yes, yes you did. We all would come here during weekends when we were kids. It was our special hangout area, especially for the two of us!" Irene said excitedly.

Kemna's eyes lit up as well as Chisakis'. "No wonder you're reading the same manga I thought of buying!"

Chisaki looked at them surprised and then laughed. "I bet if you get time to spend with your old friends Kenma, you may recall a few memories."

"Of course! That may be possible! He just needs to meet the rest of our old friend circle again, and spend some time with us," Irene replied enthusiastically.

Chisaki smiled at her enthusiasm, but then her face darkened as she gave a small sigh and shook her head. "I don't know if it's possible. You see, Kenma, my brother, and I will be leaving for Japan in three day's time."

Disbelief and anxiety gripped her heart once more, like a painful knife that pierced her heart, knowing that not much could be done in such a short time.

She uttered. "That can't be... that's not enough time."

Chapter Five
Surprise Visitors

Irene was dumbfounded. "Leaving in three days? But...why?" Kenma spoke up after being quiet the whole time.

"I have extra classes to attend before university classes actually begin for the new semester."

"Oh...." Irene thought hard. "Please give me a moment." She quickly took out her phone and began typing away.

Chisaki and Kenma watched her with curiosity. After she had finished typing, she looked back at them with a smile. "Would you both like to come over and have tea at my place?

If you do, we're going to order a takeaway, and we can maybe sit and talk about what we can do before you leave?" She gave them a hopeful look.

Chisaki grinned. "Why not? That is if Kenma agrees to it, since you guys are the ones who know each other here."

Kenma looked at his cousin and then at Irene. He smiled happily. "Well, I would like to visit one of my childhood friends, and maybe who knows?...I might just regain some memories if I get to spend time with the friends I grew up with, even if it's just for a few days."

Irene placed a reassuring hand on his shoulder. "It's settled then. Don't you worry; the road ahead of you is full of surprises. But now all that's left to do is...to wait for grandpa to come back."

Just like it was a cue, the door opened once more.

"Good afternoon. I'm back!" In came Irene's grandfather, a man who always carried a big and joyous smile on his face. "What do we have here," he said as he approached the counter and kept his bags aside.

"Welcome back, Grandpa!" Irene greeted just as joyfully as her grandfather did.

"Irene! My my, look how much you've grown! I remember you were just a little kid when you would come here to help me sell these books."

Irene grinned and gave her grandfather a big hug. Then her grandfather turned to the other two, Chisaki and Kenma, who stood up and bowed their heads in respect.

He let out a laugh. "No need for such formalities all of a sudden. It will just remind me of how old I'm getting, isn't that right, Kenma?"

Everyone looked at Irene's grandfather in surprise. Noticing their surprised faces, he laughed once more. "See? This is what I mean.

I may be growing old, but my memory is as youthful as you all are. Anyways, how have you been Kenma, my boy? Haven't seen you around since you left for Japan, and Irene has not spoken about you for a while as well. Some fight happened or something?"

Everyone was quiet for a while until Chisaki spoke up.

"It's not that sir, you see..." As she told him what had happened, Kenma and Irene went to browse for some more books while quietly chatting and giggling about the books they had read and that they were planning to read.

As they did so, Chisaki and Irene's grandfather looked at them with a soft smile on their faces. "They used to be like that as well when they were little...but maybe a little more hyper... you see, some things never change, especially when it's something that makes you who you are," Grandfather said with a twinkle in his eyes. Chisaki nodded in agreement.

After a while, Irene and Kenma returned to the counter with two books each, eyes glistening with excitement. "Alright then, you both can have those books as a gift from me. And remember Kenma, memories or not, be true to yourself. Listen to that small voice inside of you, that remains even if memories fade so that you remain who you are. Go now, you all must have plans for sure. May God bless you!"

During the journey by taxi to Irene's home, Irene showed and told Kenma and Chisaki a little more about the surroundings they passed through.

"It does feel like home here as well," Kenma said softly, admiring the view from his window.

The sun was setting when they passed by the golf course, but it was enough to see its grand and picturesque beauty. "This place..." Kenma said as his eyes widened and his mouth slowly curling to a smile. "I can somehow remember this place vaguely. I can't really tell what the memories are, but I have a feeling that we had a lot of fun and memorable ones here!"

Irene looked out her window and grinned as she thought of the past.

"We sure did! And you know what? I think I know just what we need to do, to enjoy your remaining days here in Shillong!"

When they finally reached Irene's home, they were warmly greeted by her family. Then they all sat in the living room, where Chisaki repeated Kenma's accident to them once more.

After a prayer of gratitude for keeping Kenma safe and for his recovery, they all then shared stories about the recent past and present.

As they were all laughing at the hilarious stories that Irene's father was recounting, the doorbell rang. Irene got up with mysterious smile on her face; she beckoned Kenma to follow her to answer the door.

Kenma followed her as she went to the front door to answer it. The door swung opened slowly. Kenma stood at the back of Irene, staring at the somewhat familiar faces that stood in front of him. Upon their faces were expressions of prolonged relief and disbelief.

In that moment, it was so quiet that one could hear the insect's sounds as they hovered around in the backyard. The silence was broken by excited voices of Hame, Daniel and Camie calling out as they rushed in to give him a group hug. "Kenma! It's you...you're back! You're really here with us again!"

Chapter Six

Surprise Visitors

It took quite some time for everyone to settle back down. This was understandable. After all, it had been almost five years since they had seen or heard from Kenma. And just like a miracle that greeted them this summer, a summer where they were all together, he had come back to their lives, just as sudden as he came and left in the past.

At first, they all sat in the living room to hear about the accident once more. Everyone looked at Kenma with concern and at the same time, relief in their eyes that he was able to make it out alive after the accident. After a round of heavy tea, Hame, Daniel, Camie, Kenma, and Irene went upstairs to the terrace to take a breath of fresh evening air.

It was a late evening, clear of clouds, and a thousand specks of stars twinkled brightly, decorating and lighting up the night sky.

After walking around for a bit, they all took a seat on the terrace chairs, except for Irene, who had taken her seat on a stool.

Kenma kept his stare towards the golf course, which was seen from the terrace through a peek from in between trees, shielding the rest of the view.

Noticing his intense concentration at the golf course, Irene cleared her throat and said, "So guys, as you all know, Kenma will be leaving in three days, so we must make the most of the two days and a half that we'll be getting to spend with him. Let's make sure that our plans for those days revolve around that thought. We'll visit the places Kenma has spent most his time in, especially Golf Links."

Kenma looked over at Irene with a hint of joy and excitement in his eyes. Camie nodded her head in agreement.

"Irene's right. We should maybe spend tomorrow and the morning before he leaves in Golf Links. But... what about the day in between?"

Everyone thought for a while before Hame spoke up. "Maybe we should show him his school and other places where we would hang out or go to often, the day after tomorrow? And we can eat out in the eatery that was his favourite. What do you guys think?"

The rest, along with Kenma nodded their heads in agreement once more. "Well, if we're going to his past school, we may as well do a little shopping at the mall nearby. I need some clothes and accessories, and the rest of you can also see if you want to get anything from there..." Camie said. "...And when did you take an interest in shopping? Where's that Camie we knew, who hated shopping for clothes?" Hame said teasingly.

Camie gave him a friendly punch on his shoulder. "Just so you know, I'm a grown and independent woman now, so I must take care of myself."

"Yeah right! A grown woman huh?" Daniel said, rolling his eyes and then looking away to escape his sister's glare.

Kenma, who had been quiet the whole time, started to laugh. "I may not remember the times I spent with you in the past, but I can get the feeling and sense of the times we spent together in the past."

The others looked at him with a thankful look and a bright smile upon their faces. "Don't worry Kenma, you'll have many more of those feelings, and maybe even get some memories back. I propose tomorrow we play a little bit of soccer at Golf Links, just like the old days!" Daniel exclaimed, getting up on his feet and pretending to lift a cup in proposal.

"My brother is something else at times..." Camie said, with a not so amused look on her face. But then she soon joined in on the laughter, while Irene stood up pretending to raise her glass in the air, in agreement. "I daresay, that is quite a good idea!"

Before they left, Irene beckoned Daniel to the side, while the rest gathered their things. She cleared her throat and spoke to him with a serious tone in her voice. "Daniel, remember what you told me about that incident that took place between you and Kenma before he left?"

When realisation hit him, Daniel looked away from Irene and responded with a, "Hmm."

Irene shook her head and let out a sigh. "You have to clear things out; for the both of you."

Daniel turned his gaze back at Irene and saw the determined look on her face. All he could mutter was, "Okay."

Irene got up early the next day, finished her chores, put on her tracksuit and then prepared a small picnic lunch for them. "Mom I want to go with Irene as well!" Caitlyn cried as she rushed to the kitchen where she and her mom were making lunch. "Actually Caitlyn, two of your cousins and your best friend are coming to stay over to have a sleepover for two nights, starting from today.

Are you sure you want to go with Irene and her friends instead?"

Caitlyn almost immediately shook her head and smiled. "No way! I'll be waiting for them at home!"

Irene smiled at her sister and went on to pack the picnic lunch into her bag. Just as she had finished all of this, the doorbell rang. She opened the door to find Hame, Daniel, Camie, and Kenma waiting for her outside.

"Come one Irene, let's head out!" Camie said. "Daniel and I will be treating you all to tea at the Golf Resort later."

Irene rushed back in and picked up her bag. She then went out with the rest of her friends and they headed off to Golf Links together, laughing and talking along the way. When they finally reached the golf course, they chose a spot that they wanted to have their picnic in, which was in a shade formed by group of trees.

Daniel then took out the soccer ball and beckoned the rest to join him. With Camie as the goalkeeper, Irene and Daniel in one team and Hame and Kenma in the other, just as in the past, they all began to play. It was a full 45 minutes of non-stop snatching and dribbling the ball, and attempting to score.

Camie was as good as ever with her defence, and Kenma was just as good as he was at being the most successful one to break it.

After many gulps of water, they sat back down to have lunch. "Rice and fried potato chips! Chicken curry, lentils and tomato and mint chutney! This is quite a feast you made Irene!" Camie exclaimed.

Irene replied, saying, "I didn't do it all myself. My mom taught me how to make all of this."

Daniel, who had already started to take the food, turned to Kenma and said, "You have to try everything. It's made in the traditional Khasi method, a little break from your usual food taste."

Kenma nodded as he began taking the food on his plate as well. Soon enough, all the food disappeared, and they started a little chat and a game of UNO before they went back to play.

As they were cleaning and placing the cutlery, plates, spoons, etc. back in the bag, Daniel spoke in a low voice to Kenma as he pointed to another spot nearby.

"I need to talk to you about something. Can we just stand a little further over there?" Kenma looked at Daniel in surprise, but then saw the serious and sober look in his eyes. Kenma nodded and followed him while thinking, "I wonder what is this all about..."

Chapter Seven
Daniel's Confession

Irene glanced at Daniel and Kenma, as they stood further off. 'I hope they'll be alright,' She thought.

As if it was a cue, Daniel turned his gaze towards her. She smiled reassuringly, mouthing the words, "You got this." Daniel returned a small smile of understanding back to her, and Irene started another conversation with Camie and Hame.

"So Daniel? What do you want to talk about?" Kenma asked, concerned as he felt the tension in the air, while Daniel stared into the horizon with an anxious look on his face. He then said, still looking away, "You're as good as ever at soccer."

A short silence followed. "Oh um...thank you... you're really good at it too you know."

Kenma replied, visibly confused. Daniel chuckled. "I'm just an average player... you see? In the past you and I were a part of the Pride of Shillong Soccer Club. You had us advance to the finals of many matches and even won three out of the four inter-club soccer games, and two out of the three inter-school soccer games."

"That couldn't possibly be just my effort...I..." Kenma stopped as he saw a Daniel's expressions grew sad as he forced a small smile.

"Well, I believed it was mostly you. I thought everyone could see that as well. And I'm not saying this because I'm jealous or anything.

I was actually really proud of you. So proud of the fact that when you had to leave just before the interstate games, I blew up at you."

Daniel lowered his head, looking like he didn't want to say anything further. "It's in the past...let's forget about it and focus on the present instead," Kenma said reassuringly.

Daniel gathered all the courage he had to carry on. "No, wait! I have to tell you this...this is the regret I've been carrying with me all this time. On that day you quit the soccer team, I begged you to stay and told you what I believed that we could not win without you. You told me that that was nonsense, and told me that you would always come back to play when you could. I don't know why...but I got so mad at you, I told you I'd...I'd prefer never to see you play with us again. And that was the last thing I ever said to you before you left. I didn't even give my best in the interstate matches, so to prove that I

was right, and we did lose...but we could have made it... and what's worst was, that when you never responded to us trying to reach you...I got scared. I blamed myself. I thought that the last thought you'd have of me was that I got so pissed off at nothing. That selfish of me...I..." Kenma put his hand on his shoulder and smiled.

"Look Daniel, none of it was your fault. But I'm glad you told me. Even if I may not remember any of this, I want to say that I forgive you, so you don't have to carry this burden forever. After all, I'm still here right?"

Daniel slowly turned to look at him, tearing up and smiled softly. "You're here...that's true... thank you for coming back...thank you man...thank you for forgiving me..."

They gave each other a solid hug of understanding and forgiveness and a firm pat on the back. Then they went back to the others to join them. Irene glanced at the two who were busy talking and laughing.

Camie, noticing her far off look, said, "Earth to Irene! What are you thinking about now?"

Irene shook her head and smiled softly. "Nothing... I'm glad we're able to bring back those feelings and memories of the past to life..." Irene's voice faded off as she looked up to the sky and said, "That's right... they're returning back to us."

After that, they played another game of soccer before they headed off to the Golf Resort for tea. After a lovely tea at the Resort, they all went their own ways.

Before they left, Daniel walked to Irene, who was busy gathering her things.

"Hey Irene... Thank you so much for supporting me earlier. I wouldn't have been able to do that without your help."

Irene looked up at him and smiled brightly. "Don't mention it. I'm glad that you were able to finally tell him, and lift that burden off your chest. Daniel nodded in agreement.

"You're one of the reasons why our friendship is as strong as it is right now you know Irene."

"It's because our linked memories are strong enough to hold us like this. I just do my best to re-tie the old ones by reliving them, and help create the new ones with all of you."

Exchanging smiles of understanding, and saying their "See you soon," they all went home looking forward to what the next day would bring.

Chapter Eight
Special Summer Visits

That same evening, Irene went out with her family to visit her grandparents who had prepared dinner for them. She spent the evening telling them about her life and adventures in Japan. She told them about university life, her Japanese friends, the various festivals and events she had attended such as the Cherry Blossom Festival, summer festivals, Anime conventions, and places she visited such as Akihabara, Okinawa, Osaka, and many more. She also shared about the challenges in communicating in Japanese and finding directions. She told them numerous stories; after all, it had always been a dream for her to go to Japan.

The next day at around 2:00 p.m., Irene went to put some casual clothes on, informed her parents that she was heading out with Camie, Daniel, Hame, and Kenma for some sightseeing and then took a taxi to Polo Grounds.

She waited there at the grounds for about ten minutes before a car pulled up to her, with the front and back windows rolling down as it pulled to a stop. Kenma waved to her from the front seat, while Camie's face popped out of the back window. "Hey Irene! Sorry that we're a little late. Daniel had to fill up the car with some fuel along the way after picking Kenma up. Now hop in, we've got to pick up Hame from his college next!"

They all had a fun time with some karaoke in the car as they drove off to pick up Hame. He was standing in front of his college gate holding his phone and wearing some ear-pods. They had to pull to a stop right in front of him, as he did not hear them honking at him.

"Oh there you are! Sorry, I got a little bored waiting, so I decided to listen to some songs in the meantime."

Camie quickly ushered him to get in in a hurry, as she sat in the middle of the backseat. "No need for explanations!" She said. "We have to get to the mall before it becomes too crowded!"

So, as to have a calmer Camie on their side, they decided to do some shopping first.

"Look Kenma!" Camie exclaimed as they entered the mall. "We all would usually shop from here when we were younger. Well, not together of course, but this was where most of our childhood outfits were bought from."

Kenma looked around in wonder. "It does seem familiar. The mall here isn't as big as the ones in Japan, but somehow there's this sense of deja vu here..."

Daniel and Hame then took Kenma to shop in the unisex area and then the men's section with them, while Camie dragged Irene with her to look for some formal trousers and shirts. Finally, after Camie was satisfied with the outfits she had found, and when they all had picked something for themselves, they went to the counter and paid for all the items they had bought.

"Finally!" Daniel exclaimed, drawing long deep breaths as they were out in the fresh and open area once more.

"Alright then Kenma! Now that my sister has finally settled down, let's go see the school you went to!"

Keeping their bags in the car, they all started walking to Kenma's old school, in which Hame and Daniel had gone to as well. They all stood in awe at the new modifications the school had gone through.

"So Kenma, what do you think?" Kenma looked at the school with a sparkle in his eyes.

"It's an all-boys school, isn't it?" They looked at him with a happy surprised look.

"Yes, yes it is! Irene and I went to an all-girls school just a few miles from here as well. So, do you remember coming here?"

Kenma nodded. "It's slowly coming back to me..."

Daniel then suggested, "Do you want to meet some of your teachers then?"

"It's possible?" Kenma asked.

"Of course it is! We are past pupils of the school, after all. And see over there? That's the same good old security guard. I bet he'll let us in!" And he did.

Irene and Camie stayed back and went to buy some snacks instead, as Daniel and Hame showed him around and took him to first meet the principal.

They were lucky enough to come at a time where all the teachers were just about to leave for a school meeting with the principal. Before they did, the three of them sat with the principal and some of the teachers who knew them and told them about what had happened to Kenma, in brief.

Then the Principal himself offered to take them around the campus in hope that Kenma could recollect some of his memories. For Daniel and Hame, this was a trip down memory lane, but for Kenma, it was a heavy, fruitful and joyful experience.

Many faded and clear memories rushed to his mind as he walked and looked around. He could see faces of some of his old classmates rush from here to there in the corridors, lessons being taught in the classrooms, and students eating lunch in the campus.

As they stopped by the classroom he last sat in, he could vaguely see him and Hame goofing around with the others, whenever the teacher was not there. (Daniel being a year older was not a part of his batch).

After the nostalgic walk, they all thanked the principal for his time. "It was a pleasure. I can see it in Kenma's eyes that he has gained quite a lot from this brisk walk, so I'm very happy to be of some help to my past students."

Delighted to hear the news that Kenma could in fact remember quite a few of his memories in school, they all decided to enjoy some milkshakes and cakes at Kenma's once favourite cafeteria, one of the most common places they would go eat together after school.

After some time, they decided to head back home as it was growing dark. "Looks like today brought some fruitful results, don't you think?" Camie said as they drove back to drop off Hame, Kenma, and Irene.

Kenma nodded enthusiastically. "I'm really glad to have recollected some of the memories here. Finally, this place is starting to feel like home..."

"I do wish that you were here for a few days more though... you could have remembered so much more..." Irene said with a sigh.

"I'll try to come back here when I can. And now we all can stay in touch, and tell each other our stories and experiences. And aren't you coming back to Japan once your summer vacation is over, Irene?" Irene nodded.

"See? You can tell me much more about Shillong through pictures and stories when we have the chance to meet up there... Don't worry...I'll treasure all of the memories I gained, and the memories that I made with you guys this time. I'll make sure never to lose them again."

They all started tearing up when Camie's reassuring voice filled the air. "Save your tears for tomorrow everybody! Remember, we have the whole morning to do something special together before Kenma leaves. And I heard Irene has this sorted out?"

Irene smiled and said, "She's right! Leave it to me guys. Just be in Golf Link tomorrow at the usual place at 10 a.m.!

Chapter Nine
Paper Plane Memories

The next day, Irene woke up at around 6 a.m. She looked out of her window and saw a lovely clear, pink, yellow, and light blue sky.

After saying her prayers and reading for a bit, she got up and freshened up. As she splashed her face with water, she looked at her reflection in the mirror. She could somehow see her younger-self being reflected instead. She smiled softly, remembering this was exactly what she had done five years back, before she prepared to meet her friends at Golf Links.

"Five years later..." she said as she put on some clothes for the morning's activity.

"Five years later...we're going to do the exact same thing...except this time... there are new feelings, new experiences, new outlooks, and a stronger bond."

Then, after getting ready, she took the paper bag that held the work she had made for them to enjoy that day. "And this time, for sure, I may have finally found the answer to your question, Kenma."

"Irene! Over here!" said an excited Camie, waving from the top of the golf course. Irene waved back. She could see the rest of them standing beside Camie waving to her as well. She made her way up the small hill with the paper bag clasped tightly in her hand. When she finally met up with them, she stopped to catch her breath.

"So Irene...what's this surprise that you had in mind?" Kenma asked.

Irene looked at him and smiled brightly. "Well, let me get them out for you guys." She opened the paper bag and took out a paper plane.

"Made these myself last night. We would fly these all the time when we came down here to play, so I thought that it would be a nice way to send Kenma off today."

She handed Kenma the paper plane. He held it delicately and observed it carefully.

"Paper planes..." he said as he smiled softly. Then he glanced up to the sky. "I remember seeing hundreds fly across the sky in my dream as I was unconscious after the accident. I made mine glide along with the others, but when I tried to catch it, it flew far away from my grasp...and that's when I woke up."

"Away from your grasp..." Irene repeated, her thoughts wandering back to five years back. The same soft smile. That same look in his eyes.

"These paper planes look like they carry off all those memories we made, but they don't return to us, do they? These good old times will soon be gone, just like they do, and who knows, will the memories fade away too?"

"Irene, Irene....Irene!" Irene shook her head when she heard Camie's voice as if she woke up from a trance.

"Where did you go to? You lost us there," Kenma said.

Irene looked at him and remembered what she was doing. "I'm so sorry. Got lost in my thoughts... Anyways, here are your paper planes," she said as she distributed the rest to her friends and herself.

"Whoa...you put some effort in making them. Not only did you design our names on them, but you also made them in an entirely different model," Daniel exclaimed, admiring his paper plane.

The rest of them agreed in unison.

Irene laughed. "I just had some inspiration to make this model. It's a boomerang paper plane, and suggested by the name itself, I guess you guys will be able to guess what will happen."

"Pretty cool...Let us try them out, shall we?" Hame suggested.

They all nodded in agreement.

Then they positioned their hands to prepare for take-off. When they threw them into the sky, the paper planes glided with ease into the air. Irene, who was standing next to Kenma, uttered the following words to him softly. "You were right! These paper planes are symbols of our memories, and for us as well. We'll soon go our separate ways, and fly far away from the place where we began. But look..." she pointed at the paper planes that were now taking a turn and returning back to them.

Kenma watched his gliding back towards him. "But now, we'll always be able to return back to where we began. Our memories as well..."

Irene and Kenma caught their paper planes at the same time. She gazed happily at her paper plane and spoke to Kenma once more. "They will never disappear from us. We might forget them, but know that they will somehow find their way to us again, for if our mind may not remember, our heart will never forget them."

Kenma held his paper plane delicately to his chest, his eyes filled with tears. The others had caught theirs by then, and then turned their attention to Kenma, who's tears slid down his cheeks.

"Kenma...?" the others said, confused and worried as they huddled around him.

"Oh it's...it's nothing...I'm just going to miss you all a lot. I'm so happy to have had the opportunity to spend time with all of you again!"

"Kenma...you're making us cry as well!" They cried as they took turns to hug him.

Kenma's cousins, Chisaki and her elder brother stopped their car at some distance from them and waved at them. Kenma called out to them, saying that he would come in a minute.

It was Irene's turn to hug him, and when she did, he whispered to her, "Thank you...thank you for answering my question. You cleared the fog to my thoughts..."

Shocked, Irene could not say a word. At that, she looked at him, her eyes widening in surprise. "Clear the fog to his thoughts? Does he mean, I could finally answer the question he had asked me in the past?" Tears welled up in her eyes and her mouth curved into a soft smile. She nodded slowly, giving him an understanding look.

Kenma waved at them and ran back to his car. He looked back and smiled at Irene who woke up from her astonishment. He nodded to her with understanding, got into the car, and they watched them drive and disappear into the horizon.

"He'll be back guys...just like our paper planes," Irene said, who was now wondering how Kenma remembered just that single question he had from the past.

The rest looked at her in surprise, and then smiled as they understood what she meant. They all stood there for some time, reminiscing about all the moments that had got to spend their time together just like in the past.

Summer vacation went by quite fast after that. It was now time for Irene to return back to her college in Japan. Once more, her family and friends dropped her off at the airport and waved goodbye to her as she boarded her plane. She was asleep for most of the journey, only waking up for the meals.

She had spent the previous night finishing her assignments of which she had procrastinated all along. It was then time for landing, and then time for the passengers whose destination was Japan to disembark and find their belongings.

When Irene finally found her suitcase, she headed downstairs to find a cab to take her to her college. She couldn't believe who she saw as she walked down the stairs. Standing amidst the crowd was Chisaki and..."Kenma!" She cried out with joy as she waved to them.

Paper Plane Memories

Even if we're miles apart,
Even if feelings change in our hearts,
Even if apart we grow,
Even if seasons come and go.
Even if we desire to go back to the past
To erase regrets in our minds that last.

Even if we can't see each other
Or hear our voices, sighs, and mutters.
Even if all around us things change
And memories fade,
I know paper plane memories
Will return to us again.

Think before you act, or you will
encounter regrets.
Regrets linger in our hearts and
burden our souls, and make it hard
for us to move forwards in life.

– Daniel

(Paper Plane Memories)

Even if our minds may not remember,
memories remain in our hearts,
and the heart will never forget.

-Irene

(Paper Plane Memories)

Deep in Kenma's thoughts

Faded feelings of memories,

All I remember is my family…

And the smiles they gave,

Which I wish I could see and save

Can't remember what happened

Cause the memories are darkened…

I just can't recollect them at all…

I'm still dreaming

I'm still searching

For the answers that I'm seeking

To see those smiles again

To know who I was once again

And I'll keep going on

Till I find you

To all the ones I once knew
I hope life has been amazing for you
I wonder if you still remember me...
If maybe some things remind you of me.
It doesn't matter though,
Because the love and care that you've showed
Me is leading me everyday to you,
And I know that I'll find you.

I'm still dreaming
I'm still searching
For the answers that I'm seeking
To see those smiles again
To know who I was once again
And I'll keep going on
Till I find you.

Memories may fade, but they never disappear completely. They leave behind them trails of feelings in our hearts that can be gathered to paint them in our minds again.

Let every moment you spend with a
person be one to treasure.
You may never know when you will
be able to make another one.

About the Author
Risa Tham

Risa is a sixteen year old writer, artist and now Author. Inspired greatly through literature and Manga Art, Risa devotes a lot of her spare time to drawing, sketching and writing short stories, poetry and quotations.

At school, Risa's favourite subjects are Science, English and Literature and in her free time, she enjoys playing the piano, ukulele, making animatics and watching anime.

When she leaves school, Risa wishes to pursue higher studies in the field of Science and Research as well as expanding her writing and art interest.

Follow Risa on Pinterest
@Risa_Draws

Follow Risa on Instagram
@cherryrisa_uwt

TO FOLLOW RISA'S PUBLISHING JOURNEY, VISIT:

www.youngauthoracademy.com/risa-tham

or **SCAN ME**

Printed in Great Britain
by Amazon